REA
R
THE

Falkirk Council

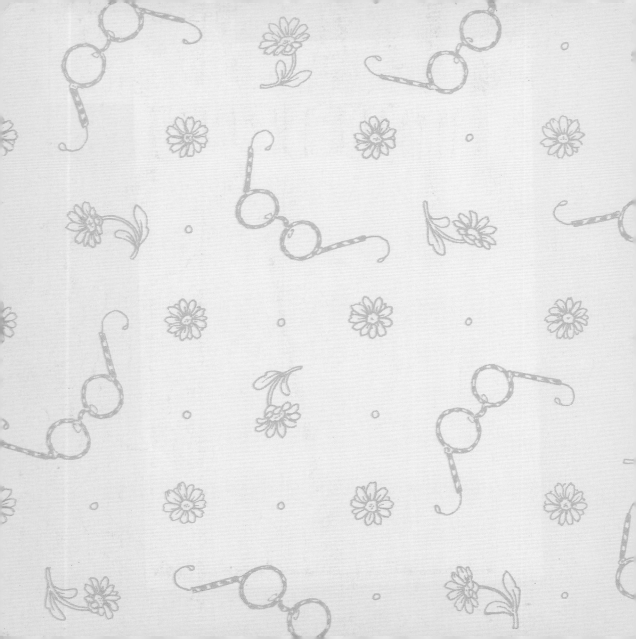

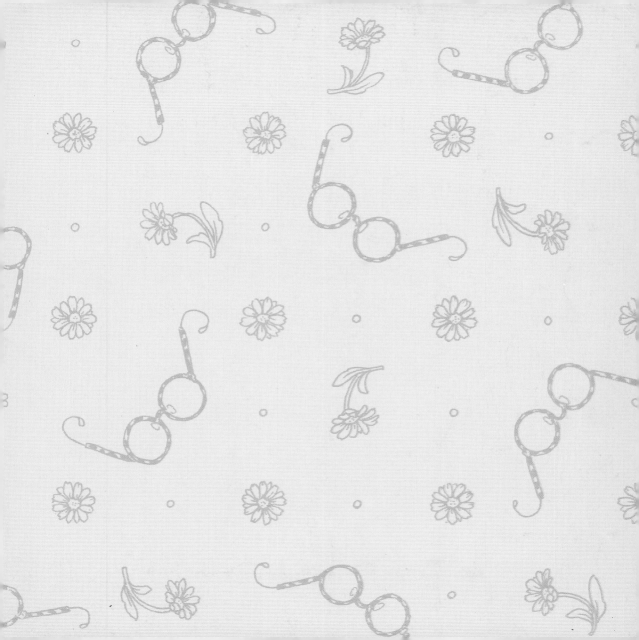

For Bethany and Jo
who gave me the idea

Daisy & Jack

THE
CREEPY-CRAWLY
COUNT

Prue Theobalds

Uplands Books

One day Jack found five slugs
eating his lettuces. He showed
Daisy, and Daisy said,
"Why don't we make a list
of all the creepy-crawlies
that live in the garden?"

"Yes, we could have a competition,"
said Jack. "Let's see who can find
the most."

Daisy had just made herself a large honey sandwich. She was looking forward to eating it, but she had to put it down when Jack brought her a piece of paper and a pencil.

"Right," said Jack. "Ready, steady **go**!"
and off he ran.

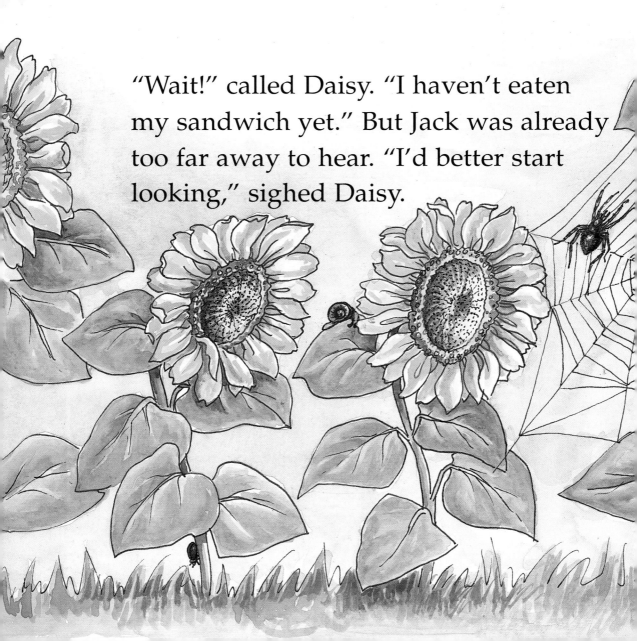

"Wait!" called Daisy. "I haven't eaten my sandwich yet." But Jack was already too far away to hear. "I'd better start looking," sighed Daisy.

She found a very large spider,
spinning its web between two
sunflowers. So she wrote
down **1 spider**, and
did a little drawing
of a spider.

Jack spotted a pink worm, wriggling out of the earth. He thought it might be two worms, because the middle bit was hidden, but it was only one.

"Surely there are some more," he thought. He poked around, but could not find any more. So he wrote down **1 worm**.

Daisy picked up her basket and found four snails crawling underneath it. They looked at her with their eyes on stalks, and she added them to her list: **4 snails**.

She was beginning to enjoy herself.

Jack lay down on the grass, and some green grasshoppers hopped right over him.

They were gone so quickly that he didn't
have time to count them. Were there
three or four? He wrote down

3 grasshoppers.

Daisy knew where to find some slugs.
She went back to Jack's lettuces.
The slugs were still there.
So she wrote down **5 yucky slugs**.

Jack was looking amongst Daisy's flowers.
He found four stripy caterpillars and
two brown furry ones
that tickled him.

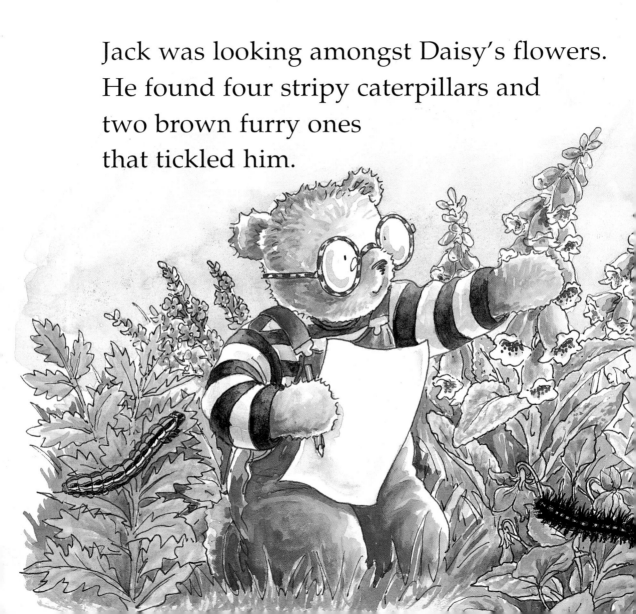

He was sure there were more. So he looked under every leaf, but he could only see six. So he wrote down

6 caterpillars.

Daisy sat down for a rest. She was pleased with her count.

Seven shiny beetles crossed the path in front of her. "Hello beetles," she said, and happily added them to her list: **7 beetles**.

Jack saw some butterflies fluttering around a pretty bush. It was difficult to count them.

"Please keep still," he begged, but they kept flying round to the other side of the bush. He thought there were eight, but he could only count six. So he wrote down **6 butterflies**.

Daisy found a ladybird crawling on her dress. She took it gently on her paw, and carried it over to Jack's beans. As she watched the ladybird crawl away, she saw that there were lots more.
She counted them excitedly.
There were at least ten.
So she wrote down
11 ladybirds.

Daisy was sure she was winning. She was hungry now, and wondered where she had left her honey sandwich. Then she saw Jack coming back, looking very pleased with himself.

"I am sure I have found more creepy
crawlies than you, Jack," she called.
"I have counted lots and lots,
at least thirty."

"Well," said Jack, "I have found your
sandwich, and about a hundred ants were
on it. So I think I have found the most."

Daisy looked sad. She had lost the competition and her sandwich.

"Don't worry," said Jack, "I will make a whole plateful of sandwiches for both of us, but I think we had better eat them indoors!"

First Published 1998 by Uplands Books
1 The Uplands, Maze Hill, St Leonards-on-Sea,
East Sussex, TN38 0HL, England

ISBN 1 897951 19 1
text and illustrations © *Prue Theobalds 1998*
The moral right of the author/illustrator has been asserted

Printed in Singapore

British Library
Cataloguing-in-Publication Data
A catalogue record for this book is available
from the British Library

also in this series

Daisy & Jack in the Garden

Daisy & Jack and the Surprise Pie

Daisy & Jack and the Circus

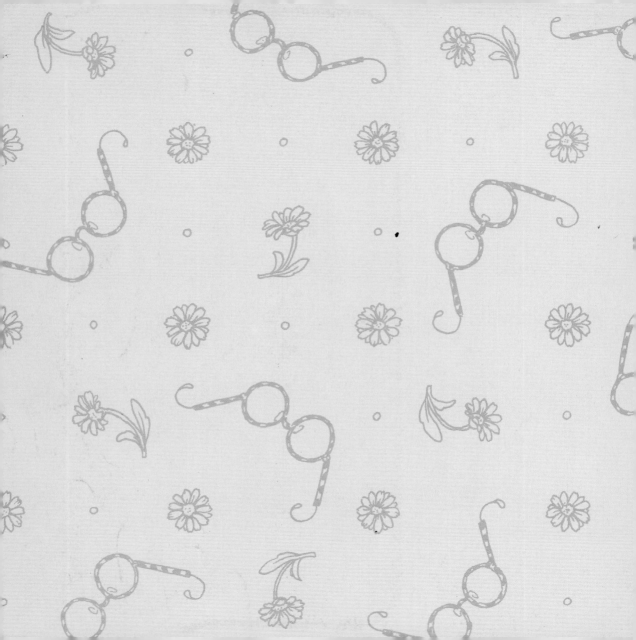

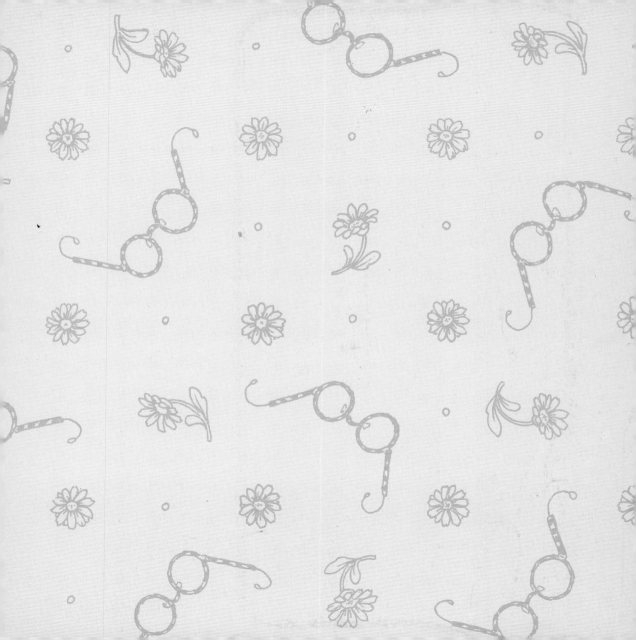